I CAN READ IT ALL BY MYSELF

Beginner Books

For Gatsby and Cleo

Layouts by Billy Steers; inks by John Lund; paintings by Diane Dubreuil.

Published in the United States by Random House, Inc., New York, and simultaneously in Canada by Random House of Canada Limited, Toronto.

www.randomhouse.com/kids

Library of Congress Cataloging-in-Publication Data
Farber, Erica. Paws and Claws / written by Erica Farber and J. R. Sansevere ; layouts by Billy Steers ; inks by John Lund ; paintings by Diane Dubreuil.
p. cm. — (I can read it all by myself)
SUMMARY: When a large green egg appears in their barn, a cat and dog investigate from where it came.
ISBN 0-679-89487-X (trade) — ISBN 0-679-99487-4 (lib. bdg.)
[1. Cats—Fiction. 2. Dogs—Fiction. 3. Domestic Animals—Fiction. 4. Eggs—Fiction. 5. Stories in rhyme.]
I. Sansevere, John R. II. Steers, Billy. III. Lund, John. IV. Dubreuil, Diane. V. Title. VI. Series.
PZ8.3.F21667 Paw 2001 [E]—dc21 99-057748

Printed in the United States of America January 2001 10 9 8 7 6 5 4 3 2 1

PAWS AND CLAWS

Erica Farber and J. R. Sansevere

BEGINNER BOOKS
A Division of Random House, Inc.
New York

I am a cat.

My name is Claws.

My partner is
a dog named Paws.

We watch the farm.
We watch the house.
"Hey, Paws, wake up!
Look, here comes Mouse!"

Mouse says, "Hey, guys,
please come with me.
There is something
that you must see!"

Inside the barn,

there is a rat,

a duck, a goat,

a horse, a bat . . .

. . . a sheep, a lamb,
a pig, a goose,
a cow, a hen,
a mule, a moose.

And on the straw
by Horse's leg,
what do we see?

A big green egg!

The egg's so big.
The egg's so green.
It's like no egg
we've ever seen!

So Paws and I
check out that egg,
that big green egg
by Horse's leg.

We tap it twice,

roll it around.

And that is when
we hear a sound.

The sound is small—
small as can be.
The sound of some
small he or she.

"What do we do?"
ask all the guys.
All eyes are on
the egg surprise.

“We’ll hatch this egg.
That’s what we’ll do.
We’ll sit on it.
First me, then you.”

So first I sit.

Then after that,

Lamb sits on it,

then Bat,

then Rat.

Mule gives a try,
but he's so big,
we yell, "Watch out!"

Next up is Pig.

Horse has a go.

And so does Moose.

And Cow

and Sheep

and Goat

and Goose.

Paws goes next.

And then goes Duck.

When it's Hen's turn,
she says, "Cluck! Cluck!"

We leave the barn,
just Paws and me,
to find out whose
this egg can be.

We start with things
that we have seen
around the farm,
things that are green.

We ask a frog.
She shakes her belly.
"Frog eggs," she laughs,
"look more like jelly."

We ask a snake.

She shakes her head.

"My eggs are white,

not green," she said.

Turtle eggs
are white and round
and mostly buried
in the ground.

The time has come
to take a look
in what we call
the Big, Big Book.

I take it down.
I read and read.
I try to find out
what we need.

And there it is.
I yell, “Yahoo!”
In the big green egg
is a baby emu!

“What’s an emu?”
Paws asks me.
“A kind of bird,”
I say. “Come see.”

We head back out.
Paws gives a call.
Here come the birds,
some big, some small.

I tell the birds
what they must do
is look and look
for an emu.

The birds tweet, tweet,
which means, "Okay."
Then off they fly.
They fly away.

Back in the barn,
we find—guess who?
None other than . . .

. . . Baby Emu!

We all cheer,
“Hip, hip, hooray!
Baby Emu
hatched today!”

Here comes Blackbird.
He has some news.
He found a farm
with some emus.

So Paws and I
and Emu, too,
all hit the road
for Farm Emu.

Mom and Dad
are filled with joy
when they see
their emu boy.

Our job is done.

We say good-bye.

We head for home,

just Paws and I.

Who knows what our
next case will be?
Tune in next time
and you will see.